FRANCESCA LIA BLOCK

how to (un)cage a girl

JOANNA COTLER BOOKS
An Imprint of HarperCollins*Publishers*

HARPER TEEN

HarperTeen is an imprint of HarperCollins Publishers.

How to (Un)cage a Girl
Copyright © 2008 by Francesca Lia Block

Library of Congress Cataloging-in-Publication Data
Block, Francesca Lia.
How to (un)cage a girl / Francesca Lia Block. — 1st ed.
p. cm.
A collection of love poems for girls.
ISBN 978-0-06-135836-4 (trade bdg.) — ISBN 978-0-06-135837-1 (lib. bdg.)
1. Teenage girls—Poetry. 2. Love poetry, American. 3. Children's poetry,
American. I. Title.
PS3552.L617H68 2008   2008000629
811'.54—dc22   CIP
                                                                              AC

Typography by Nancy Goldenberg
1 2 3 4 5 6 7 8 9 10

First Edition

for the girls

CONTENTS

PART 1

years at the asylum

thirteen: the little oven

i thought my teacher was a nazi
with hair slicked to the side
short and germanic
he lectured about hitler
spittle
in his voice
boys with greasy scalps
drew cartoons of me
with a witch's nose
my body was so thin
i had chopped off
my pretty brown hair
my skin charred and blistered
red bumps broke out
there was blood between my legs
is this junior high school?
hell?
or somewhere worse?

fourteen: europa

in florence i saw the most beautiful
    man in the world
standing by the botticelli
birth of venus
as if the painting had split open to deliver him
he even smiled at me
white teeth golden cheekbones

on the top of the hill was *david*
huge marble perfection
exposing his penis to me alone
can you imagine in america
god made flesh
but without the blood or loincloth?

by the trevi fountain in rome
pan himself made an appearance
curls and a gap between his teeth
when he grinned at me

a hairy, cloven mystery
lurking
in his jeans

the hotel overlooked a square
the walls were thick and ghost
white with moonlight
shadows streaked the room
i woke to hear my father growling to my mother
"get onto me"
and saw their bodies moving in the bed
beside my tiny single
cot

that was when i too turned to stone
my mouth sealed shut

they packed me up and took me off to greece
to introduce me to some marble goddesses
without pubic hair
as if that might make me feel better

my parents with good intentions
rolled their new caryatid onto the white sands
    of the beach
a million perilous pulverized
petals of pearl
the water was such a sheer blue
you could see right through it
to the wavy patterns on the ocean floor
like aphrodite's hair

i knew i should be grateful for this opportunity
to see the birthplace of the goddess
but how could i ever speak of it?

the greek boys came to play with me
they frolicked around
brown and curly full of life
when night fell and the ouzo glasses
    lit up like lanterns in the taverna

my mother said, "kiss him, darling, it's easy
so natural"
and i thought to myself, not with lips of stone
dear mother
not with lips of stone

fifteen: the canyon

steamy hot night in the eucalyptus rainwater-forged
canyon my friend and i discovered a ruined house
the wildflowers growing over the foundation and a
silver ring with a king a queen a snake and a rose
then as we walked home a boy on a motorcycle
zoomed to a halt leonine face tall rambling body
somehow the next thing i remember he was sliding
his hands up and down my legs i hadn't shaved and
was prickly but he didn't seem to mind later we
kissed in my friend's shag-carpeted bedroom with
the water bed and beanbag chairs his hands moved
higher i wonder where the parents were i know a
few months later my mom dropped me off at his
apartment in west hollywood his mother was gone i
imagined she was very beautiful young and blond
maybe in the sex industry no father and i was
wearing tight jeans and a floral crepe blouse with
fake pearl buttons and when he kissed me he said i
tasted like garlic from the bagels i'd eaten with my

parents at brunch this he minded though he did let me touch his penis and then i left that is all i remember though i think once in a disco parking lot i saw him again but nothing happened why do i remember only certain details and really the main question is where was my mother?

popular girl

who are you?
(you are not like me)
where do you come from?
who are your parents?
what does your mother look like?
and your father—how does he make money?
to pay for those jeans? those shoes?
and what about your hair
it is all about the hair
you cannot be one without good hair
with frizz or split ends
what kind of shampoo do you use?
what does your hair smell like?
it is long and shines
is there a rule about pimples?
you never have pimples
why not?
are your hormones different?
are you an alien?

what are you going to be when you grow up?
are you still going to be beautiful
with good hair?
even when you die?
are you still going to be mean?
are you going to be a beautician, wife or realtor?
cosmo cover girl? queen? genius?
will you get married and divorced?
will you have popular daughters just like you?
and why are you mean?
why does mean = popular?
you know about sex, too
how do you know so much about sex?
i can see it in the way you move
who taught you?
did your mother teach you?
just by being sexy?
is it an innate thing?
what do you think about
alone in your bed at night
are you ever alone?

or do boys come in throngs through your window
popular boys with good hair and an innate
    knowledge of fucking
what is your bed like?
do you have lots of stuffed toys
    and shiny throw pillows?
do you write poetry in your diary?
is it anything
(like mine?)

are you popular because you are
a heightened version of the norm?
if that is the case and high school
was an insane asylum
who would rule?
you
(or me?)

sixteen: first time

my boyfriend took me to a party after hiking
i heard someone say, "she's got that outdoorsy look"
i was dirty
and had on hiking boots that he had waterproofed
so the pretty soft suede turned dark and dull
there was a beautiful blond girl
dressed for a party because she knew she was going
    to a party
and not on a hike
my boyfriend said good night and put me in the car
then he went back in for some reason

i knew with a woman's knowing
though i was a girl
that he was going to try to get a phone number
he had photos of girls all over his desktop
a collage of images
my boyfriend and i hadn't fucked yet

i was his younger virgin
part of his collage

when we finally did it
after a dinner of rare meat
at a fancy restaurant
the flesh stuck in my belly
i wore a strapless flowered sundress
we went to his gay friend's home
and my boyfriend sniffed some amyl nitrite
     when he came
he noticed a tiny hair growing near my nipple
"you better do something about that," he said
i was so young
too naive even
for tweezers
but not for shame, of course
that comes early

after, i paraded in front of my friends
in a green knit dress and high-heeled shoes
i'm a woman now
my boyfriend and i broke up a few weeks later
goal achieved
i had one night of grief
but the virgins, my friends, were sadder

i realized he had been
part of my collage too

seventeen: war

my girlfriends and i put naked barbies
    in the strawberry jell-o
ken had a mohawk, kilt, tiny earring and eyeliner
we girls danced in the living room
and had a cake fight
there were no boys by that time
just us all in shiny pink
waiting for something to happen
not expecting it to be anorexia or cancer or never
    seeing one another again
or war
we were like those naked plastic dolls
swimming in a soft sweet rosy sea
while ken waited outside
untouchable
hoping no one would mistake him for g.i. joe

eighteen: monster

just when i thought i had escaped
the hatred of my body
my dad told me he had cancer

after, i went running
down the street
my face bloated red with tears
the boys screamed ugly from the car
when they saw me

i never understood
i had made my father's disease
into my body
ugly

even after his death
she stayed with me like a gargoyle
only now have i begun to slay her
with the second corrective plastic surgery

poetry yoga therapy
glycolic peels
expensive haircuts and supplements
psychics, massage and shoes

that clinging figure
with the horns and forked tongue
i forgive her
she was trying to save me
in her way
make his disease something
i could point to
see, here it is
help me
kill it

nineteen: the asylum

when she thought of it she didn't think
of the mental hospital that the city was known for
she thought of cresting the hill in the vw bug
falling into a valley of twinkle lights
she thought of beaches
fields of strawberries fragrant in the heat
as jam as cakes baking
surfer boys with sun-bleached curls
and sons-of-dentists teeth
she was one of five l.a. girls
on their way to a party
in tight striped pink tees and tighter jeans
drunk on keg beer
dancing to the go-go's
making out with the boys
in their parents' strange, clean,
    bleached-sheet bedrooms
weak-limbed weak-willed with lust
thinking it was love

only later

when the boys didn't call

were hospitalized for cocaine

or married the beautiful spanish sisters of the boys
    she went to college with

when she baked her skin in the sun until it blistered
    and bled

and her father told her he had cancer in his bones

was she vaguely aware

of the asylum

a myth of love for girls

when the father died
    parts of his body were scattered
to the four corners
his eyes went north
his hands went east and west
his feet went south
the daughter spent twenty years searching
    for the parts of him
she found a man who had her father's eyes and saw
her the way her father never had
she found a man who had her father's right hand
    to hold
her the way her father never could
she found a man who had her father's left hand
    to paint
her the way her father never did
she found a man who had her father's feet
she stood on top of this man's feet

as she had stood on her father's feet
    when she was a little girl
but not after that
and she and the man danced this way
the girl loved all the men equally
    and she was no longer lonely
but her heart was still broken
into four pieces
so she wept and wept and the men
bewildered by her tears
drifted away
but after some time her tears mixed with the earth
and became clay
and she formed the clay into a man
who was not any part of her father
when she kissed his mouth he came to life
and together they roamed the four corners
    of the earth
both whole and alive

and in the sky were birds
and underfoot was grass
and to the east rose the sun
and to the west
came the moon

PART 2

in the lair of the toxic blonde

lost in los angeles

running from the green-eyed lady
i got lost on the freeway in l.a.

i saw the mexican markets
i saw the train tracks
i saw the old bridge and the cement river
i saw the vast expanse of grayness
leading nowhere
i saw a dog zigzag thirsty

i thought of the woman with her eyes
    like cold green glass
and her smirking smile
how she tried to eat my boyfriend and my mentor
    and my house

i thought, what has happened to my city
with its roses and angels?
i thought, what has happened to my boyfriend
who was bowling with miss green eyes
    just the day before?

after she ate his heart
he handed mine to her on a china plate
just like the one she used to serve him meat
in my vegetarian kitchen
and then left

so i dug in my purse for my cell phone
and i called my friends
sara and sera and maria
and they looked at maps and told me
    which way to turn
and they helped guide me home

it is good to see the sadness of my city
without roses without angels except the ones
    disguised as your girlfriends
it is good to get lost in her
it is even good to let envy hold your heart
    in her mouth
but if you don't give in to her my darlings
she will release you
she will spit you out

toxic blonde

you are those little craftsman houses decorated
with strings of lights and candles in paper bags
lining the path to the backyard where beautiful
lesbians live in silver airstream trailers and bonfires
burn and old dogs try to steal the macaroni and
cheese and cookies off the table you are forgotten
kings of the punk rock scene wearing circle jerks
buttons and speaking in scottish tongues and you
are hot loud-mouthed big-breasted blondes in pink
fur coats and fetishistic shoes taking photos of
everyone and making them laugh and you are
guava cream cheese pastry bakeries and movie
theaters with golden egyptian gods and the
hospital where i was born and where my dad was
treated for cancer and you are lights tumbling
down the dark hills like bits of crushed glass and
you are shoe stores called lush selling four-inch
cork-soled metal-studded round-toed suede slip-on
platforms that will certainly this time make me feel
beautiful at least for one day and you have made

me feel like shit all these years when all you loved
were your blondes with small noses and big boobs
and you have made me cry countless times because
you were synonymous with death by car crash or
melanoma and you have made me feel like a freak
writing poetry in a land of actresses though now
i've found your poets and they invite me to their
gatherings and ask me to sign old copies of my
books and if i had been in new york i would have
been one of a million neurotic jewish women
writers i would have not learned to forgive myself
in a room full of girls with perfect tans i would
have not learned to walk on such high heels i would
not have found my ex-husband and therefore my
children who can't be mad at you because they
know nothing else i would not dance outside under
the almost invisible stars i would not be thinking
so much about plastic surgery i would not have
burned my skin to blisters in your sun i would not

have been able to write forty-five poems in as many days and i would not have been able to say i have been able to write them because of this fertile flowery toxic blonde that is how

media queenz

we liked winona because she seemed intelligent
   and sensitive
with good taste in men
and a bit of a goth sensibility
julia annoyed us we didn't trust her voracious smile
natalie too perfect slightly cold
nicole, salma and gwyneth breaking our trust
when they donned fake noses and eyebrows
boned up on their suffering
to play our saints
though we loved angelina
in spite of the fact that of all of them
   she had the most potential
to destroy a woman's life

it was not the careers so much we envied
not the rich and famous men
(except perhaps for johnny
who tattooed her name but left anyway
to marry a french model)
it was not the chance to portray all kinds of women

on a giant screen
it was the doe eyes the big lips the skin
    fine grained as porcelain
it was the dresses shoes the grace
the way our men said, "i used to want a movie star"
turned away from us in the drugstore
to stare at magazine covers
even while we were buying condoms
even while we were bleeding

where were our pradas? our pouts?
    our captivating glances?
only later we would grow up
and realize that these women were just women
they ran from the altar they stole
    someone else's man
they shoplifted they got loaded they tattooed
the wrong name on their bodies

then we could be grateful
we are pretty enough stylish enough
we are unscrutinized
we are loved

duty: for sofia

she was a princess of the holy wood
her parents brought her to a jungle
    when she was little to sit
at the feet of a prophetic madman
when she was older she performed on the stage
the crowd put her in the stocks and threw vegetables
at her da vinci face
her brother the prince drowned in the sea
she married
a man everyone called genius it seemed like paradise
she wept
alone in her villa while he flirted with actresses
she made
art won acclaim and her husband's jealousy he left
she wore
only short black or white dresses
some full some slim and elegant black flats
was named best dressed on every list smiled quietly
and like a cat

told a story about marie crowned queen at nineteen
dressed in magical shoes
showered with jewels
and cake not loved properly lost in a castle
    of gilt dreaming
of the natural world making babies finally beheaded

but this princess keeps dreaming her next dream
she has a lot of stories still to tell
she knows that in times of danger it is up to the girls
to overcome humiliation and grief even decapitation
and save us

vampire in the city of lost

once there were these two girls
 who were really bored
and they put on their shortest skirts
 and highest heels
the ones that made their toes bleed
and they applied perfume to all their pulse points
and they went out into the shiny city
where they met this tall vampire with a shaved head
and a body tattooed with the stories of the centuries
and the face of a matinee idol
please please drink our blood they begged
tossing their hair away from their long swan necks
please make us into the immortal dead
and the vampire said
oh no oh no you silly girls
that is not really what you want
it might look fun but actually it kind of sucks
but we are bored, said the girls

we want to wear the fashions of the future
we want to have countless lovers
and most of all we want to stay young and beautiful
    forever
but the vampire gave the girls a lecture
    about global warming
and the unfathomable hours of the walking dead
if you think you're bored now! he said
he bought them kir royales and kissed them chastely
    on the lips
so that their mouths went numb and tingly
    for a moment
and then he left
the girls hobbled home on their bleeding feet
and they thought about that handsome vampire
sitting up in a tree
watching the deserts flame around him
or sailing on a melting ice floe
while the polar bears died
and the girls were glad to be alive

and they were glad they would eventually die
and after that they always turned off
all the lightbulbs in the house
when they went to bed
hoping they were helping the planet
and, secretly cloaked in darkness,
that the vampire would come back

l.a. bacchantes

yxta and francesca decided to start a clique
for frail but surprisingly strong fairies who had lost
    their way above ground
for burned mermaids and sick vampire girls
for wild wolfish women with sharp teeth and leaves
    in their hair
for women who had been raped
and women who had never been touched
for women who had been devoured limbs eaten
and women who had sucked the blood
    of their passive mates
for ladies who had at one time or another considered
    themselves hideous monsters
and who had at other times blinded their lovers
    with goddess glory
for smart hungry sad creatures who disguised
    themselves as women
and wept in secret because they did not look
    like supermodels

for loud lascivious funny femmes fatales
who wanted to eat flowers and whipped cream
and dance on the tables
smash things and wear pieces of the chandelier
    for jewelry
fuck satyrs and lick dark chocolate off
    each other's bodies
be worshipped online and flirted with
    at parties and glimpsed
in the pages of *vanity fair* in an article entitled
    "l.a. bacchantes"
but mostly just needed each other

yxta and francesca had always desired world peace
    and profound romance
but this clique wish seemed somewhat selfish maybe
    superficial and greedy
they did not yet know how significant it was
no different really from the peace and love
    they had been born wanting
and perhaps would change not only themselves but
the world

people's park (escape to the north)

stay away, they warned her
she watched from a distance as those others
    crossed the threshold
a giant swaddled as a mummy
a dreadlocked satyr mumbling
curses to the blossoming trees and garbage
a fortune-teller who sheltered
    a whole family of fairies
under her skirt
a witch with a young woman's body
and the face of dried apple
rice grain teeth like the dolls the girl used to make
    with her mother
some days she yearned to leave the icy marble halls
where no one knew her name
and join them
leave the plates of greasy food
that congealed their fats at her abdomen
leave the cruelly beautiful blond boys and girls
in their polo shirts and top-siders

drinking kegs and fucking and ripping
fancy paper off the walls
of their grecian mansions
it would be better to sleep in mud
eat roots and flowers
discarded crusts and the coffee
the vendors left out for her
after all, who had that giant been before?
lurching down the street as if his feet
    were burned stumps
he reminded her of the injured dragon
    in the dream last night
afraid until she gave him water and kissed his lips
that did not scald her
she bargained with them i will stop eating i will
    sleep in the dirt
sleep out all night on the cold marble steps
i will write poetry about you revealing
    your true selves
but they would not let her in

she returned to a city they never even dreamed of
where the homeless lived in cardboard shacks
and had forgotten they were ever
something else

like pretty

what would it be like if i thought i was pretty
what would it be like if i carried
    that knowledge around
like i do the knowledge that i am a writer
pretty like peonies pretty like satin pretty
    like the child i was
would i speak to you differently
would i be healthier less stressed
less worried
would i buy more shoes or fewer
would i be more or less afraid
of death would i find something else
to hate about myself
would i get this jealous
when your eyes aren't touching me
in this city of movie star beauties

would i be able to write such raw
    and seductive words
would you have fallen in love with me sooner
would i have frightened you away
before you had the chance?

my love

my love is undisciplined
unruly
tangled
she is always hungry
my love wants sweet and savory
baklava and stuffed grape leaves
mango smoothies and avocado sushi
carrot cake and butternut soup
my love does contact dance with strangers
and sweats between her legs
she discusses auschwitz with men in galleries
and thinks she was once anne frank
my love is clairvoyant
she can read past lives the way she reads books—
haphazard, invasive and devouring
my love sometimes wishes she were a lesbian
but she is unrelentingly heterosexual
my love loves babies
pink cake boxes

penises

sheer sequin covered tunics

shoes

(currently she is on a dogged internet search

    for pink satin platforms)

my love's nickname is l.a.

she is extravagant

guileless

with no knowledge of spells or witchcraft

if my love had her own body

she would look more like angelina jolie

than like me

i can't blame her for feeling cheated

by the body she's stuck in

my love wants to change the world

she thinks she has so much to give

not realizing how much she takes from others

my love is loyal until she senses rejection of any kind

then she flies like a bird but has less memory

    of where she came from

i would like to protect you from my love

she is the creator and the destroyer
she wants so much from you
she would kneel at your feet
and clutch at your heart
that's the way she does things
but i am her slave
no longer
i will witness
the way you tilt your head
undulate your shoulders
fling me onto your back
cradle me
hold me upside down
whisper love lyrics into my ear
carry my pink purse
not recall it all
run away
call me anorexic

tell me your ex-girlfriend was the love of your life
that you will never love anyone that way again
and my love and i will simply watch and wait
until we discover
who you really are

PART 3

love poems for girls

for the girls

i searched for him in the dancer dark
and i prayed for him in the new moon park
and i called to him with my poetry
but perhaps i was not yet ready
because he did not come
instead the girls danced along with their arms
    full of flowers
songbirds on their shoulders
they made me strawberry smoothies
    decked with parasols
and photographs of fairies
and they told me that i had helped them
now we want to help you they said
their tears were like the rain that washed
    grief's memory
from my back step
we put on my grandmother's tattered silk kimonos
and my eight-inch platforms
took photos of each other laughing and glamorous

and ate red velvet cake on rose petal strewn plates
they were my sisters and my daughters
and in those moments i forgot he was not there
and i forgot to fear
that he might never come

pain is like an onion

remove one layer and the next is there
keep peeling, my beloved
peeling and chopping
putting in the pan
fry it to translucency
and eat it
let it digest
it's only been a year and a half
since he took your heart from your chest
peeled it chopped it fried it ate it spit it out

eventually a new one will grow back
eventually
the tears
will stop

ornate

what makes you think you can be so ornate,
    my darling?
even your name means princess
even your hair with its long black curlicues
even your eyes such dark blue as to be violet
what makes you think you can use such words
paving your poems with jewels and lights?
and your heart!
desiring that much
as if it were a victorian valentine in your chest
polished pink quartz chambers
or even an elizabethan pomegranate rose
a rococo clock all golden and decked with cherubs
ornate and especially your sorrow
what makes you think?
this is what—
your birthright

your sorrow a guide to lead you on your journey
it says go forth be bold be brilliant
    desirous of what is yours
for this is who
you are

teenage fairy: for m

i didn't feel like i was enough
so i changed my nose
and i changed my skin
and i changed my bones
and i changed my blood
and i changed my home
and i changed my love
and i changed my clothes
and i changed my belly
and i changed my friends
and i changed my mind
until the man i wanted came to me

but after a while he left anyway
and i was alone with this new self
we slept in our bed with the roses she and i
and we sat by the pond waiting for water lilies
and we wrote poems to each other
and we photographed ourselves in the mirror

and i was still lonely, rummaging in the bed
    in my sleep
seeking someone who had never been there at all

then this big-eyed, long-legged
fourteen-year-old fairy wrote to me
and she said she didn't think she was beautiful
and i told her not to let her pain confuse her
trick her into thinking untruths
and i told her that her pain was not her fault
but that she could use it to make beauty
instead of to hurt herself

and that night i slept peacefully
in my own arms

the little mermaid: for ama

you dreamed of gills so you would not drown in the
sea of him you dreamed of a tail instead of legs to
keep him out you gave up your voice hoping that
would bring you the casing of green and silver scales
layered over hips shining your long legs fluttering
into fins where once were feet in shiny mary janes
you had the right hair already white lighting your
face you had a strand of your mother's pearls
beneath your pillow you had the right dreams of
blue-green water faraway coastal cities where you
belonged instead of those parched towns where the
men hunted creatures like you and mounted them in
their living rooms but you did not get your fish tail
and your voice was gone even your legs didn't work
quite right anymore you hobbled away from home
leaving a trail of blood and pearls men and women
followed you wanted to touch you and you let them
hoping one would know the spell but it was not until
you reached the pacific and flung yourself naked

into the surf your hair writhing like seaweed on the
water your eyes turning greener with the reflection
your breasts and between your legs finally your own
this is when you grew gills to really breathe this is
when you grew a tail prettier than your best french
gown this is when you found your scream your
poetry your voice

neptune's daughter

confused by her fish's tail
she wanted legs to walk with
a womb to birth a child
she blamed her father for this impediment
to her true nature
something she had inherited from him
like the potential for illness
oversensitivity
a tendency toward depression
but oh he had also given her so much
twinkling eyes an insatiable
love of life
the ability to turn sorrow into incandescence
you are an artist he had told her
though he had never shouted
what she really needed to hear

and what, given her tail, was questionable anyway
you my darling, cherished one
are a beautiful
woman

miniature mouse

miniature mouse knows these things
she is still young enough to remember
that once she had a boy attached to her body
their very viscera entwined
their kiss just a natural proximity of lips
and even the roses and the little animals
were further extensions of them
so when they were ripped apart it hurt her more
than those who have utterly forgotten
and she must record the travesty of separation
again and again
the amputated limbs
the gouged out eyes
the double heart torn asunder
this is the task of the young, the artist
who remembers

for valentina

value your musical name your fashion sense
    your strength
your light and dark your uncanny ability to appear
    resurrected from the dead
believe him when he tells you you are beautiful
it will only hurt you both not to
(it is true besides)
dress as hard-core as you fancy or as sexy
wear black while your skin has enough light
    not to absorb it
show off your belly and your breasts
    as much as possible
someday when you have wrinkles
you may want to wear the clothes you sneer at now
spit swear dance fuck just don't smoke cigarettes
    and do wear sunscreen
(i wish i had listened to opinionated old women)
don't be afraid to age

you will be more self-assured thus just
as fabulous as now
(except that then you will know it)
hold on to kind men don't let them go
searching for the ones who will prove to you
    the untrue things
you believe about yourself
choose to believe the ones who see
    what you may not
choose to believe in your own myth
    your own glamour
your own spell
a young woman who does this
    (even if she is just pretending)
has everything

valentina screama

valentina is a doll with a spun sugar pink
    pompadour
streaked with white lightning
eyes like ink melting pooling from the pupil
    to the iris
to the slashes of lashes
marilyn monroe skin
dead-girl blue fingernails
she comes dressed in a replica of the egyptian gown
that a female vampire wore in the original *dracula*
long silvery pleats skimming her hips
    and a midriff top
held with a giant scarab
but in her black coffin-shaped box is a pair
    of tiny black converse
torn black jeans and a joey ramone t-shirt
for her more casual moments
valentina also comes with a tiny silver pistol
that shoots red glitter hearts

like a glam goth cupidette
she has another secret weapon too

every girl wants a valentina screama doll
every boy secretly does too
they don't know that at night she steps
	out of her black box
and watches you sleep
if you have been cruel or false
she bites you with her other secret weapon
the charming fangs hidden behind
	her mysterious lips
it is not an unpleasant sensation
more like a tingling chill
like a spider bite that swells with venom and itches
	to remind you
of who you might someday be

as i remember it: for lily

because now as i remember it
there was almost always a smell of flowers in the air
all i had to do was read poetry and write
run through the low green hills
once a pack of us walked across town
    to a chinese restaurant
ate mu shu vegetables the thin pancakes the thinly
    cut strands of cabbage and carrot
and tofu the lovely plum sauce
a dark moonless night
the porch lights of the old houses on
the leaves whispered threatening rain
but we got home dry
my boyfriend stayed in my dorm room he was sweet
as kind as a girl
on weekends we took a train into the city there was
    music there were white wine beat
poet bars with sawdust on the floor candlelight
    through the glass melting golden

colors everywhere pink taffeta thrift store dresses or
    cream lace ones with blue
ribbons spreading out around me like petals
turquoise satin pumps with pointed toes
john doe and exene signing my t-shirt
chinese pastries and vases decorated with dragons
    and peonies

a beautiful black-haired girl
who was studying medicine and painted lilies
emerging from darkness
bought me sushi shaped like flowers
told me she had a crush on me
though i didn't know how to reply
just as i didn't know how to stay with that sweet
    sweet boy
though when i dropped to ninety-five pounds
he put his woolen arms around me
and held me close
trying to keep away the cold
and my father's cancer
though we never spoke of it

for karen: whose last name i can't recall

i was afraid she would take my boyfriend away
the one with the wounded looking mouth
pale child's eyes with starry lashes
like he'd just come out of the bathtub
he wore a white shirt, levi's and black shoes
    wrote me poetry
we went to hear punk bands in dark basements
    in the city
stayed in a hotel gray as the mist gray as doves
i was convinced he would fall in love with her
her white blond hair her germanic features
that was before i had discovered my secret
wound the story of a triangle my father loved
    my golden mother
my mother loved my father i dark haired
    and invisible
so i starved myself as the excuse
and ran away before the boyfriend
with the hurt mouth the star eyes could

and when i returned to berkeley a year later
he was in japan meeting the woman who would later
    be his wife
and the blonde?
she was in a class i had and when we shared
    our poetry
hers was about a thin girl in cowboy boots
and an antique peach silk slip
that showed the outline of her legs beneath
a girl so much more fragile than the poet herself
who stomped fiercely in black
both of them lost in a land of earthquakes

she was the second person ever to make me poetry
maybe i had it all wrong
maybe i was the one who was supposed to fall
    in love with her
and now i can't even remember her name

joanna: wood thorn fairy

skin white roses hair like red
she chose a body that was still small
to help her remember who she really was
she refused to walk
danced everywhere
on solid feet
the men she found could not keep up
staggered and fell
behind
so she waited
skipping down the streets of the big
    dangerous citadel
rearranging the silver bells
and cockleshells
and pretty maids in rows
in her apartment near the park
of angels and rapists
birthing books instead
they sat at the table

drinking tea from china cups
with faces and feet
they slept in the white four-poster bed with her
they danced with her in the evenings before the fire
and read her their stories at night
later, she began to give
birth to other things
tiny tables and chairs
made of twigs
acorn beds with mossy coverlets
miniature bouquets of violets
in miniature baskets
life-sized paper dolls with their souls
painted on their torsos
these reminded her of who she was
and kept her happy for a while
until a plane crashed through two towers
and the terrorized
city
burst into tears of flame

he had twinkly
eyes and a gap between his teeth
was a bartender downtown
where bankers and publishers soiréed next door
to the corpses of cows
he poured her a drink and told her
     about his paintings
he danced the whole dance with her
and then another and another
loved her soul, her voice, her breasts, her legs,
     her skin, her hair
but by now
under the roses her hair was silvery
     and her eggs mostly gone
this did not mean a baby
was not possible
they had to feed it
it cried just like a real one
they called it boo and bobo and baby bee

it needed to be suckled and nurtured
read to played with
loved until it grew
and learned to dance
when they lay together in rooms
    overlooking the park
the sweetness nestled between them
they remembered the secret green world
    they had come from
and knew they could return to it
as only elementals can
they forgot for a moment
that the city was
or ever had been
afire

selene: the dress with the cigarette burns

remember college
did you once wear silk or satin
slips with black boots?
did you once smoke
in the basement of a new haven punk club?
did you ever burn your skirt?
precisely
just so
little holes gaping prettily
around the hem
like mouths?

now you like to curl up at home
sober and barefoot
making little girl dresses
(sunflowers
or ballerinas)

the little girl
you didn't have but are
is angry at daddy company
where people lie and cheat and steal
she wants to hide inside and sew all day
in a room sea green
with a sphinx machine
she wants to make curtains
long and floaty
to hide her from the world

but selene you will put on
pearl gray suede platform heels
strut in to daddy
in the silver dress you made
slashed with precision
burned with grace

how to become a priestess

pain can destroy or create

once you got in trouble for not wearing your jacket
    in the cold
as if he were concerned for your well-being
burning your fingers with his cigarette ash
punching you in the jaw
and raping you on the floor
of the bathroom you had scrubbed for him

now you have fairies scurrying in your garden
drinking from the rhododendrons
spirits hide in the jack-o'-lantern the solstice fir
press themselves flat as dried petals in the books
bring toadstools and feathers for your altar

you have lilies and goddesses
a candle full of secret oils and gems of your intention
you would have used a stick but your friend gave you
an athame sword for divination
sharp enough to kill a father

gretel finds her way

gretel was abandoned by her mother
so she never knew she was beautiful
her eyes simultaneously green as oceans
and red brown as earth
her smile incandescent
her body all lean pale muscle forever dancing
you should have seen her legs
her hands described the air sculptural
    and masterful at once
as if the statue came to life to carve itself from stone
but gretel thought herself small and freakish
    a goblin
she went into the dark meadow
scattering parts behind
telling herself it was a way to get back
though actually it was a form of slow suicide
her eyes rolled off like marbles
her teeth chattered in the grass
her white hands and feet lay severed ancient artifacts

fragments of a goddess
that someone would then have to resurrect
from their imagination and dreams
oh gretel do not despair
do not stuff the hole in your face
where your pretty mouth once was
with bewitched cake
marzipan gumdrops taffy sugarplums butterscotch
chocolate creams cherry tarts
this will only make you forget for an hour
then you will weep again and your stomach will hurt
no witch wants to shove a child in her oven
    and eat it
she would rather have a fertile womb to birth one
kiss it and hug it and feed it wholesome foods
witches are cursed and they are not
    so much different from you dear gretel
wandering lost and afraid with your male self
    detached from you
just as lost
and your female self grown wicked and insatiable

come here dear i have a thought for you
why don't you tell us your story
dance it and put it on a stage
with low hung swaying lights
girls and boys dressed for a soirée
in black and white satin tuxedos
red lips and glowing eyes
you do not have to rip off your pretty skin
    to show us your innards
when you dance for us
we know that swirling there is chaos and also stars

collage

she used to wear vintage dresses over her bikini
    and flip-flops
ride to venice beach to read virginia on the sand

she used to make collages with images of the virgin
mary and roses she used to write poetry

she went to a ballet high
school and could have died
for beauty
not only from the eating disorder
but from the words of the mean mistress

she found her mother on the floor of the bathroom
with a bottle of pills
but still alive

her roommate in college was raped
    and brutally murdered
another friend died the same way at a different place
    and time

her terror turned into worry
about small things
like the overgrown cuticle on her little toenail

she married an artist and went to clubs
with scrawls on the walls called art
kept her collages private
intricate and glistening as hidden body parts

her husband stopped having sex with her
she doubted her poetry
because a mean bulimic woman
told her she couldn't write

she took up african dance and then brazilian
because they honored rather than denied her ass
helped her heal her marriage
and the scars of ballet and anorexia

she danced into the arms of the drummer
they could have been brother and sister
he read her a poem on their first date
she was still married when she made love to him
left her husband almost right away
married again in the hills above malibu
dancing on the crest above the sea
    with white flowers in her hair

she gave birth to two children
decorated her house in pink and green velvet
teaches thirteen year olds literature every day
comes home and cooks dinner every night
writes her books on the weekends

the war makes her so mad she needs meds
she's okay though
her husband still wants her whenever possible
still reads her poetry aloud

she has finally discovered
the brutality is not inside of her
however there are many roses, there are altars,
    there are stories

miranda

blonder
stronger
smarter
but motherless
you were easy prey
to monsters

who knows how vile
what they did to you

no wonder you sought out the most beautiful man
as a means of escape
told him your whole nightmare tale

it was not your fault he ran
any girl in your situation needs a friend
after the dollhouse was smashed

but miranda you got off
the island
before it was too late
you gathered your shards your twigs
your surf pounded shells
lipsticks and flower petals a shiny beaded earring
	wild parrot feathers
many books
made a nest of words
in which to lay your eggs

your father may burn
his books of magic
and abandon the sprite once locked in a tree
but not you miranda
not you

fairy sisters: for sukha

it was hard to understand what they called reality

babies died
men left
mothers grieved and turned to pills
wars existed
wars?
religion itself
baffled us

even mortality seemed wasteful and ungenerous
inherently imperfect
there was so much to do

that was why we obsessed on pretty things
frozen yogurt or candy
dance and poetry
golden shoes with pale suede platform soles
twinkling necklaces
essence of vanilla and lavender

in a base of wild white sage
and vervain
reminded us of where we had come from

then there were the elf boys
of course we wanted them
desperately
their minds their hearts their seed
they recognized us and made us feel less afraid
but they were lost, too

above ground

needed weed and solitude
instead of so much sugar
kisses
and adornments

the world looks different
without the comfort of soil and roots
the place where flowers are
born

happi happi joy joy and sad in hawaii

happi wanted to take sad to hawaii
happi's friend had gotten her two free tickets
happi had many friends and they were always
     giving her things
happi wanted to see sad basking in the sun
healing the scars on his back
sipping a fruity drink
and watching the sunset on the waves
but sad had never heard that bit of folk wisdom—
if you knew you were going to die tomorrow
wouldn't you feel stupid for not eating more
     birthday cake
or, it should be added, going to hawaii?—
so sad did not go
happi was quite adept at traveling alone
she packed a bikini and some shades and a lovely
     printed cotton sundress
and got on the plane by herself

it is important to note that happi had not
    experienced any less pain
than sad
she had just learned the lesson about birthday cake
    much better than he had
he needed to learn a lot
in spite of his excellent taste in film and literature
and his swooning, crackly-voiced compassion
and as the sun turned the sea into
    a tropical mixed drink
and the stars came out above the cabana
happi realized that she would wait for sad
    for as long as it took
but that in the meantime she would not stop eating
    birthday cake
or traveling to exotic places
or dancing with her friends
pleasure and sweetness and love

yxta

this fairy had been so close to death
she had dined at his long metal coffin-shaped table
and sat on his belly
and he had kissed her charming lips
but then he had let her go
she sang him such sweet songs
about the most devastatingly beautiful
women of history
and she danced so seductively
like a little tibetan goddess with many arms
and also she had this man who loved her so much
so bravely and selflessly
how could death
thus spellbound
take her away?
so the fairy was released from death's
    gripping fingers
and she went back to the man who loved her
    so much

and she sang him her songs
and danced him her dances
and when she smiled she showed off
her tiny charming fangs
but the wings were definitely a problem
sprouting from her sharp white shoulder blades
little feathery things
and she tried to pluck them out
because who would take seriously a vampire
    with wings?
but they kept growing back
no matter how hard she tried
reminding her of who she really was
and would be for all eternity

titania

somehow there on the street the only two
eyes turned at the same moment mouths dropped
open

titania
on a dirty sidewalk yellow roses angel curls
black rhinestones white wrists

my heart just hours before cracked
so wide by grief
born of fear
in you walked

both of our defenses gone we saw
as if for the first time
and forever
how did we lose each other for so long?

where were you?
at the birth of twin nieces

day and night
on a stage naked and mythic in madonna's
    extensions
you were there
when the planes hit the towers
ran through the city past the people dressed in ash
the panicking cops the silent hospitals
    without bodies to be saved
you fell into your sudden lover's arms
moved back to the country bought a trailer
a loudspeaker so everyone could hear
sat inside with your red lipstick mouth
your cacao bean vanilla voice
talked to everyone heard their stories

it was a little like when you volunteered to massage
    rescue workers
the only thing that healed holocaust survivors
    they say
was touch and talk
where was i?
having babies

trying to shelter them from 9/11
trying to teach them to live love instead of fear

what was wrong with me?
jealous of your hair your voice your strength the way
    you spoke to my man
even as you gave me pastel thong underwear
decked with bows
and told me people like me should have babies
to make the world a better place

titania why
should i be surprised
at what happened?
even the greatest of cities have fallen
to their knees when fear rules
love

and they have been
temporarily at least
reborn

the face

at first your face frightened me
your face was the face of the girl
    i'd always wished to be
your face
i thought wrongly
was the face of the girl who never felt pain

if i could have worn a mask
    it would have been your face
if i could have had one wish at fourteen
it would have been your face
if i could choose between the gift of words
    and your face
i would choose the latter

your face looked the way i felt inside
i understood gossamer and rose petals
light on shallow water
mossy glades and the stained glass
    of butterfly wings

but my face was wrong
not mine
not what i felt inside

and you came up to me with that face
and i was afraid
and then you said, thank you
thank you for that story

it was the one about my botched nose job
my acne scars
my face-hate
you looked at me and your eyes had golden rings
like lakes made from compassion's tears

you came to my house to write with us
you said you were a model
i tensed at the word
afraid of it as if you had said you were
a dog catcher or a cigarette manufacturer

but you brought gifts

bags of silk dresses
sea shells
cherries
your open heart
your wounds
they made you even more exquisite
you said sweet words
sweet as the cherry shape of your mouth

you came again and again
you said kind things to all of us
you brought cushions and fairies and goddesses
you called me part of your star

i look at you sitting on my couch
writing in your journal
your sheath of gold now twisted up
onto your head
with one flick of your wrist
cat eyes blink and kitten nostrils flare
fairy chin and cheekbones
a dryad's petal lips and eyelids

thank you for taking away my fear
we are not so different little cat goddess
fairy woman
wood nymph
star sister

valentine

my friends stitched it up with golden thread
like a red
satin pillow they gave me other whole ones too
roses and charms and red candles
milagros to repair the real one
they told me i was no longer allowed to give it away
a pretty pin cushion
a piece of mexican folk art
a hundred beating poems left unanswered
like a thing to wear around the neck
they said you must heal we will protect you
but i sat weeping at the computer
    forging ahead anyway
with the small stitched thing struggling in my chest
it knew that it had needed to be torn
so that it could recognize and receive
    the hundred kindnesses

traveling across three thousand miles
    at the speed of light
a storm of petals and beautiful words
    and tiny hearts to keep it
company

the three graces

the three graces, sera, sukha and yxta, came to bless
    my home
they lit one golden candle
made by brooklyn witches
and three black candles
made by midwestern witches
the gold one was to warm
the black ones were to ward off grief

grief had ventured into my house
tentatively and with his eyes closed
he would not sit on the bed but went instead
into the backyard
the lily pond disturbed him
though the roses were worse
and the picket fence made his skin crawl

grief's face was calm
his beard was trimmed

he wore a black bandanna on his head
he looked well-rested and composed
though he had once held a dead baby
    in his small hands
and fallen to his knees in tears
    before another woman
but tonight grief watched me crying in the garden
and asked me to accept what i could not understand
and told me he needed his space

he waited until i said, go now
and then he got up and ran through the house
disappearing into the night forever

i went to my computer and emailed all my friends
help me, i said
he has abandoned me, i said
not realizing i had banished grief

sometimes i see him through the sliding glass doors
that lead from my bedroom to the garden

his profile drawn by the shape of the dark trees
the head of a satyr
but the black candles still burn
and the roses keep blooming irrepressible
grace dances with me in the front room
grief is not welcome
here

a half imagined history: for o

1970
you are born to a girl
a boy inside a girl
i am sitting in front of my teacher with my hands
    on her big belly
feeling the baby kick

1975
you want a penis so much it makes you cry
i have cut off all my hair in a bad pageboy
i have braces and pimples
i am grinning as if i am happy

1982
are you starving yourself?
i am

1985
you are running and jumping

powering through so you don't have to think
about what you are not
but it is who you really are
you just don't believe it yet
just as i don't believe i am beautiful

i am wearing pink and black creepers from london
my hair is bleached blond
i stomp around the campus searching for someone
but all i find are the bronze sculptures in the garden

1986
what have you lost, darling?
my dad dies of cancer

1989
are you still in hospitals?
are you drawing out your sorrow?
my first book is published
i wear a sheer lace blouse and a kimono fabric skirt
my boyfriend leaps around the room flirting
    with everyone

we will break up in a few months
it doesn't sound so bad but i won't kiss anyone new
    for years

1993
you are in manhattan
i kiss a scorpio and move to the desert

1998
where are you now?
i am getting married
we will divorce a few years later
it's worth it to have our children

2000
i have one

2002
i have two

2007
i am about to turn forty-five
you are drinking too much
you are so beautiful it makes our solar plexuses ache
all of us who click on your pictures obsessively

i have found you!
at last
i missed you

forty-five thoughts for my daughter and my virtual daughters

i always believed if i had blond hair, pixie face,
     big breasts
everything would be all right
not realizing that culturally idolized beauty
is not only foolproof
but potentially dangerous

if you believe in your own unconventional beauty
when you are young
you will accomplish twice as much and suffer half so

turn off lightbulbs and light a candle

walk don't drive

plant a tree

wear sunscreen

dancing is an antidepressant

kindness is the new status symbol

every day please try to eat something green
    and something orange
that grow out of the ground

tell me how mad you are
    that your father and i parted
i will always listen
    though i can't ever take away the pain

expectations are for what you yourself create

they rarely work when applied to others

turn off the television

tv is a depressant

yoga is an antidepressant

don't feel guilty about wanting pretty things

they would not be so alluring
    if you weren't supposed to want them
just don't value them over compassion

use your words even when you are a grown-up
and people no longer think it is entirely acceptable
when you say, that hurt my feelings

if you can digest chocolate eat it sometimes

same goes for ice cream
(i don't really need to tell you those things do i?)

do your homework because it is part of the game but

don't spend too much time worrying about grades

fall in love with someone kind who loves your body
    and your mind

if you have a dream that won't let you go, that
    tickles your solar plexus, heed it

turn dark feelings into paintings or poetry
    or dancing

music is a kind of food

if you are sad talk to a happy woman who loves you
it will always help

move your body when you are sad or angry

avoid the following:
genetically modified ingredients
parabens
sodium lauryl sulfate
mercury in certain fish
neurotic thoughts about food
(is that a contradiction?)

love your curls though they tangle
your pale skin though it can burn in the sun
your nose though it is broader than some
your sturdy legs and feet

forget barbie she does not possess imagination

remember you are a botticelli angel

the planet we live on is perfection

love her like a goddess

love yourself as her daughter

there is a planet full of different kinds of beauty

the idea that only one type of woman is beautiful
is blasphemy

of everything i brought to the world in these
    forty-five years
you and your brother are by far the most astounding

because of this i will always love your father

matter never vanishes, only changes

remember that when someone you love dies

your round head on my breast when you were born
    is the memory
i will keep with me when i leave this body

when i am gone i will still be near you

this is how i know: when you were born
    it was not a meeting
but a reunion

how to (un)cage a girl

longer hair bigger breasts smoother skin
flatter stomach whiter teeth smaller nose
if you worry enough you won't have time
or energy to see
what really is

what could i have learned
if i didn't live here in this cell?
where could i have flown?
how would i have grown?
if i forgave this shell?

oh, my body
let me cradle you like my girl's
her long limbs spilling over
or folding up like silk
her gold-tinged curls
ringleting my fingers
her eyes the blue of sorrow
and hyacinth

oh, my body
when you are at peace
rocked here to sleep
as if by a mother
as if by a lover
who sees your flushed skin
the grace that you're in
the gleam of your hair
the green of your stare
then this soul can fly off
to understand pyramids and time
history
electricity
technology
symbology
that all of us are one
that all of us are love